all the beating hearts

julie fogliano

pictures by
cátia chien

NEAL PORTER BOOKS

HOLIDAY HOUSE / NEW YORK

each day starts
with the sun

and hopefully
something to eat

and something to wear

and possibly somewhere to go

or somewhere to stay

and the day will be full
of what daytimes are always full of:
work
or play
or work AND play

and sometimes
nothing much at all.

and we will watch the clouds
from where we stand

and the birds will come and go

and some things will grow
and overflow

and other things
will turn into something new

or shrivel up
or fade away

and some things
will die.

and along the way
there will be love
with its arms
wrapped around us tight

and some days we will curl up
and wish to be
any
other
place

and sometimes
we'll be filled right up to the top
with the feeling
that everything is exactly right

and the night will always come too
and then we will
find our sleeping place
and maybe we will read
or sing

before we close our eyes
and drift
into a dream

(hopefully a good one
but sometimes not)

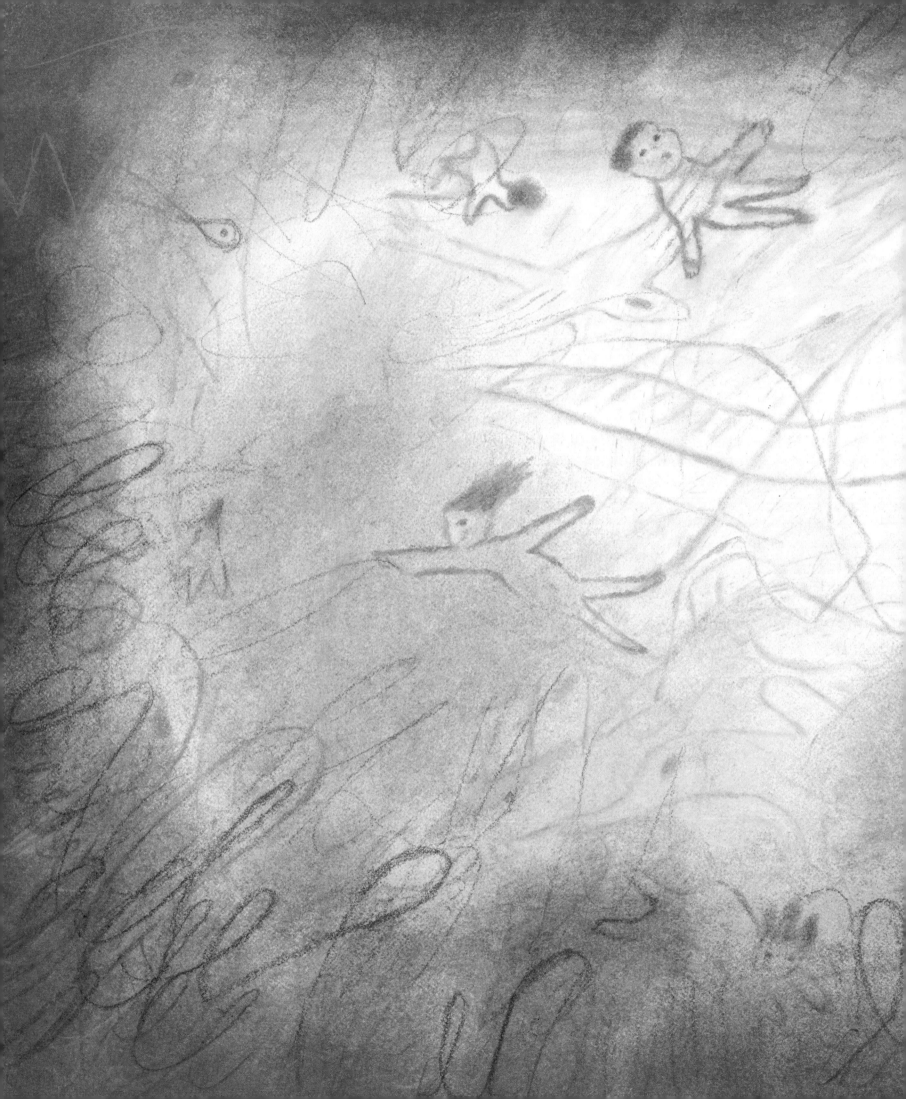

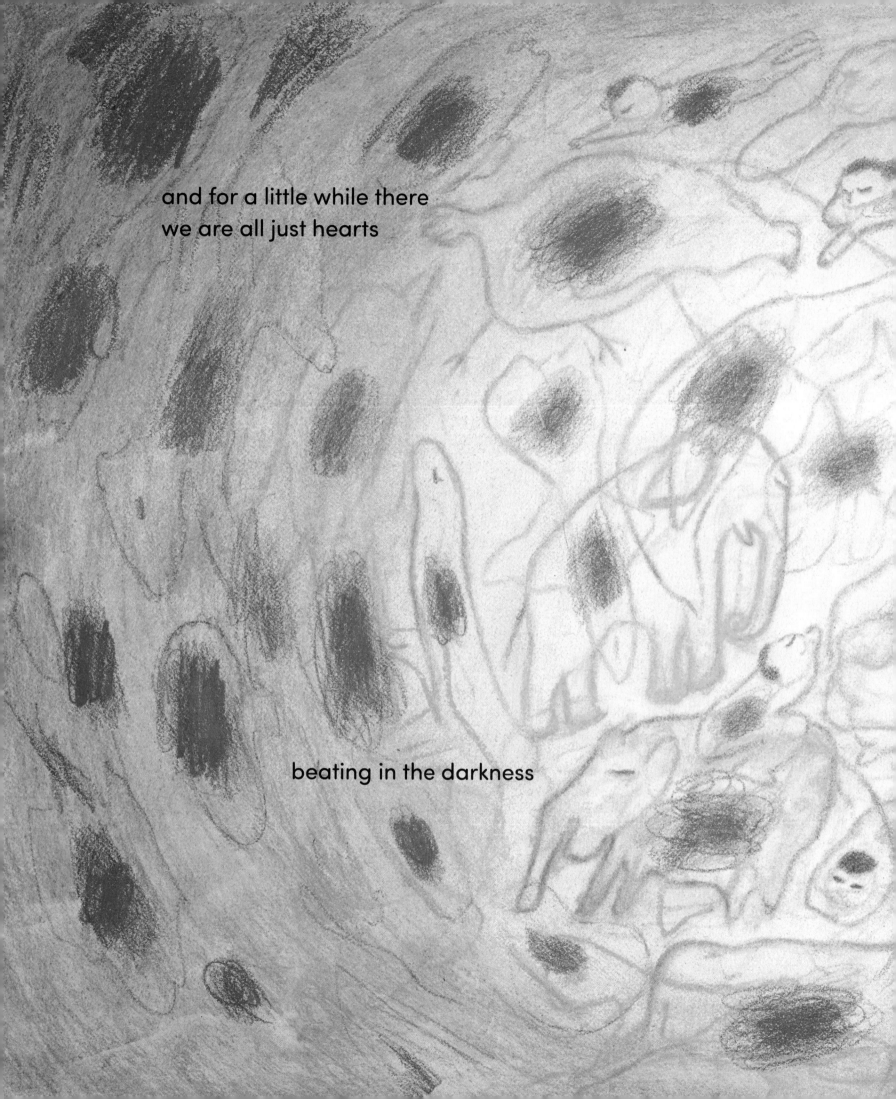

and for a little while there
we are all just hearts

beating in the darkness

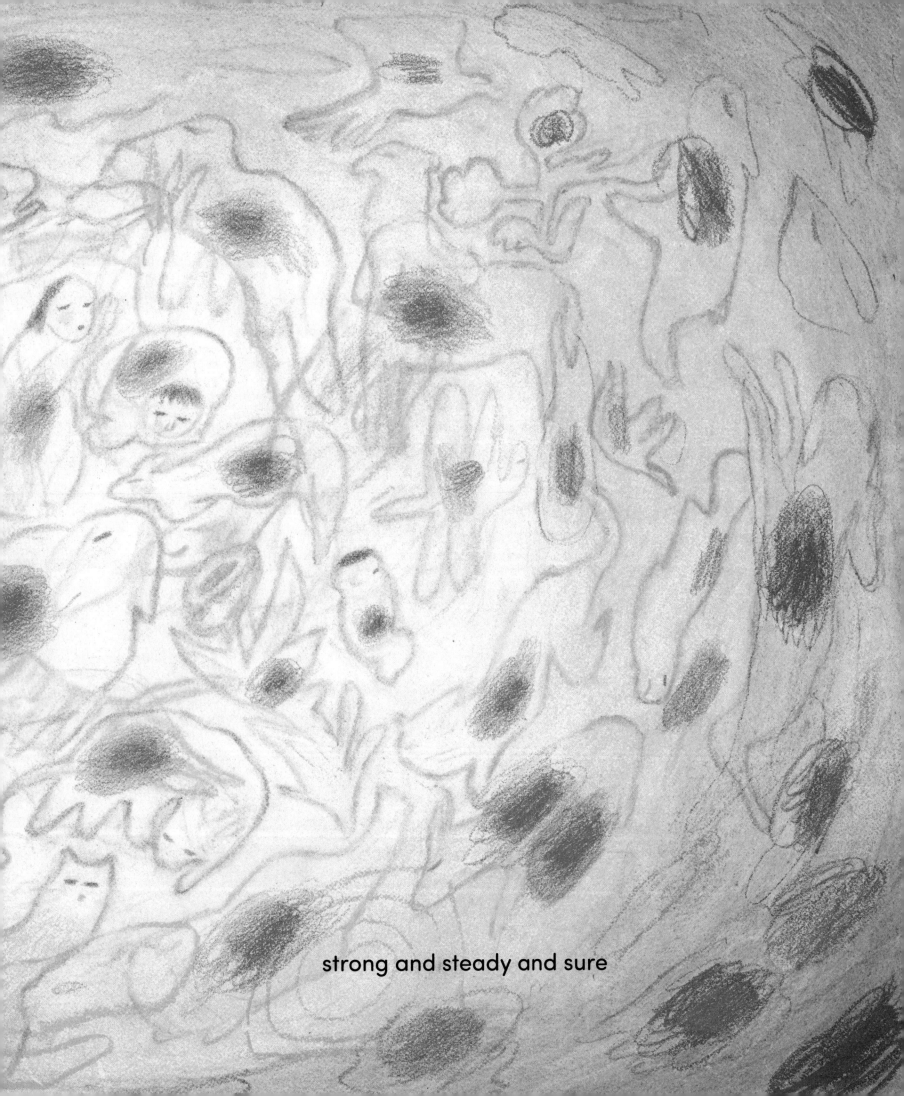

strong and steady and sure

each beat
a reminder
that we are here
and alive
together but apart
the same, but exactly different.

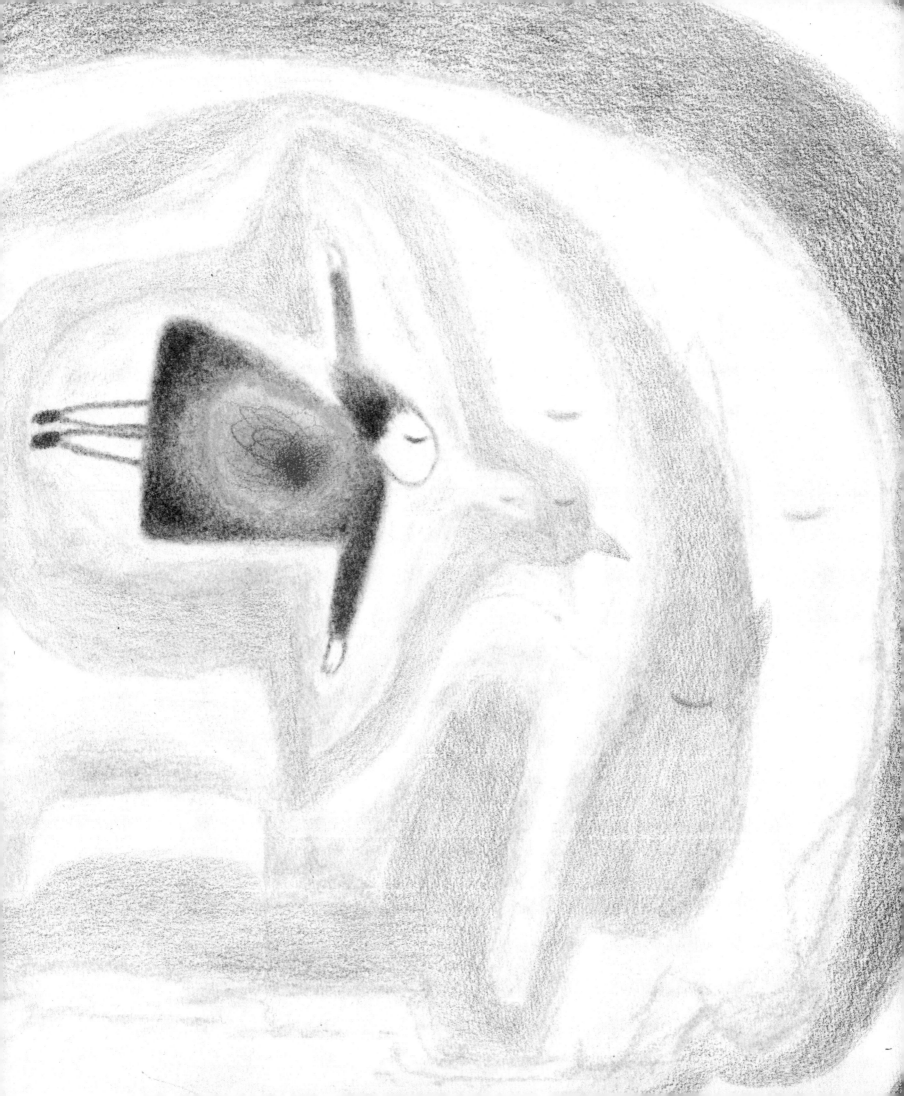

and for just a little while

there in the dark

that is all
we need to be.

and then the sun
shines us
into a brand new day

a day that is bright and blinding and full

and everyone is busy being
everywhere and everything else

and all those beating hearts
are still there, but struggling
to be heard above it all

each beat
begging us to remember
that we are already
everything we need to be

here and alive
together but apart
the same
but exactly different

and nothing
needs to be heard
except for our beating hearts

strong and steady and sure.

for clio, nico, enzo, and josh,
the hearts of my heart —j.f.

To my teacher, the late venerable Thich Nhat Hanh,
for helping me find my way back to my beating heart —C.C.

Neal Porter Books

Text copyright © 2023 by Julie Fogliano
Illustrations copyright © 2023 by Cátia Chien
All Rights Reserved
HOLIDAY HOUSE is registered in the U.S. Patent and Trademark Office.
Printed and bound in September 2022 at Leo Paper, Heshan, China.
The artwork for this book was created using pastel and colored pencils.
www.holidayhouse.com
First Edition
1   3   5   7   9   10   8   6   4   2

Library of Congress Cataloging-in-Publication Data is available.

ISBN: 978-0-8234-5216-3 (hardcover)